I0742089

Oops! All
YAMAS

ANATOMY OF A
YAMA

COMING IN AT A WHOPPING 6'9" AND 420 POUNDS, YAMA IS THE BIGGEST WOLF BRO YOU WILL EVER MEET! HE CAN BE A BODYBUILDING JOCK, A HORNY WEREWOLF, A GRUNGY ROCK STAR, OR EVEN A DEMON OVERLORD. HE COULD BE ANYTHING! LIKE BARBIE!! ER... IF BARBIE POUNDED DUDES ON THE REGULAR...

OOPS ALL YAMAS

An art collection by Yama

x.com/yamasmut

wolfyama.bsky.social

Published and distributed by

www.furplanet.com

Adults Only

DAMN, I STINK!
LOL...
WHAT?? YOU WANNA SNIFF, BRO?
THOUGHT YOU'D NEVER ASK ;) GO FOR IT!
No amount of Axe is going to help here...

YAMA
FUCK, THAT'S HOT !!

That poor towel is hanging on for dear life

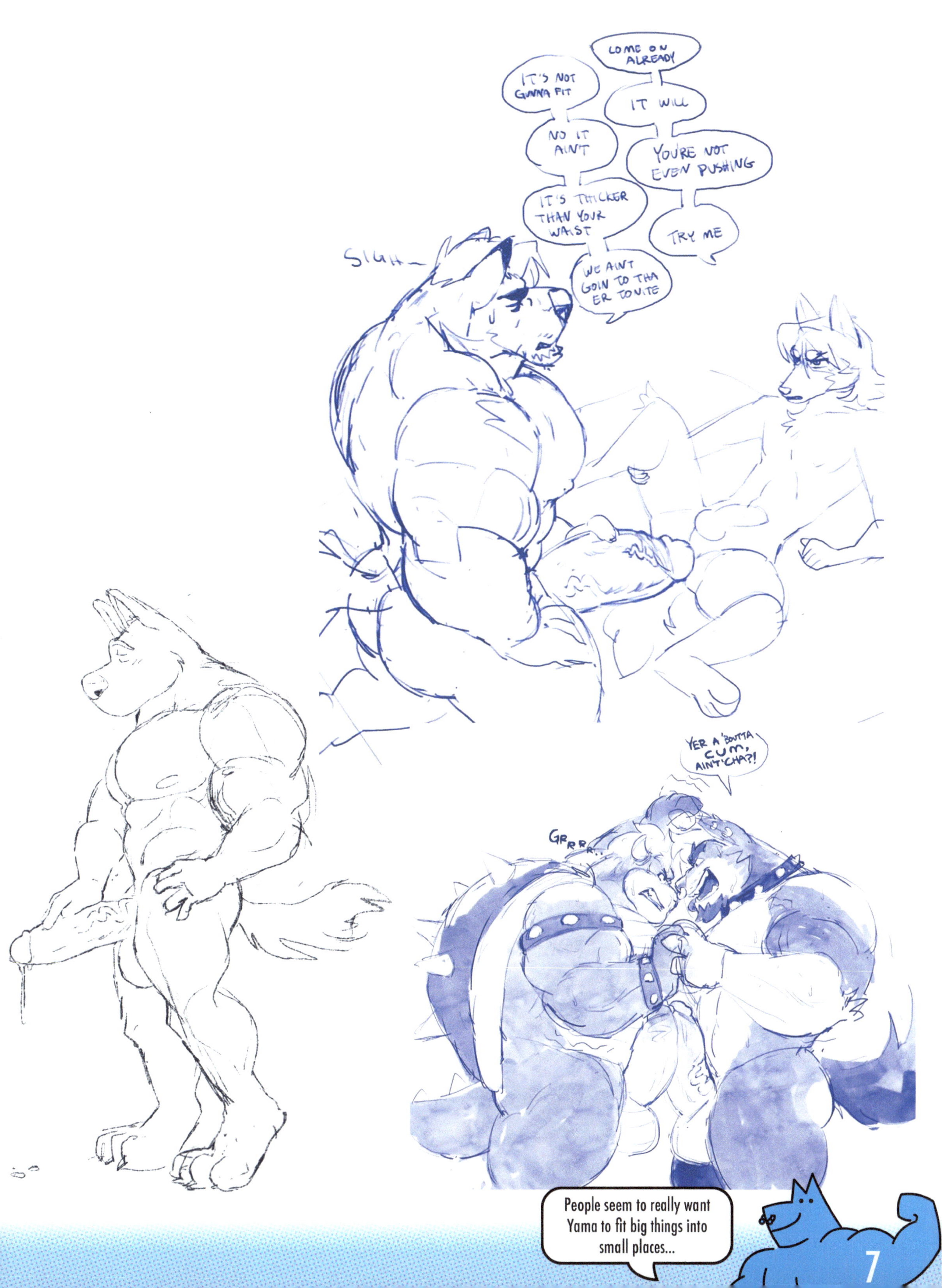
COME ON ALREADY
IT'S NOT GONNA FIT
IT WILL
NO IT AINT
YOU'RE NOT EVEN PUSHING
IT'S THICKER THAN YOUR WAIST
TRY ME
WE AINT GOIN TO THA ER TONITE
SIGH_
YER A 'BOUTTA CUM, AINT'CHA?!
GRRRR...
People seem to really want Yama to fit big things into small places...

Blake gets lucky with one night with Yama ;3

YO WHAT THE FFFFF—— UUUUUUCK!!!
THAT'S RIGHT, PUP. CUM ALL OVER THAT HANDSOME FACE. MMM... STILL GOIN' AFTER YOUR 16th SHOT, WOW
YAMA 2021
God they're spilling yogurt EVERYWHERE. Somebody has to clean up, y'know!!
9

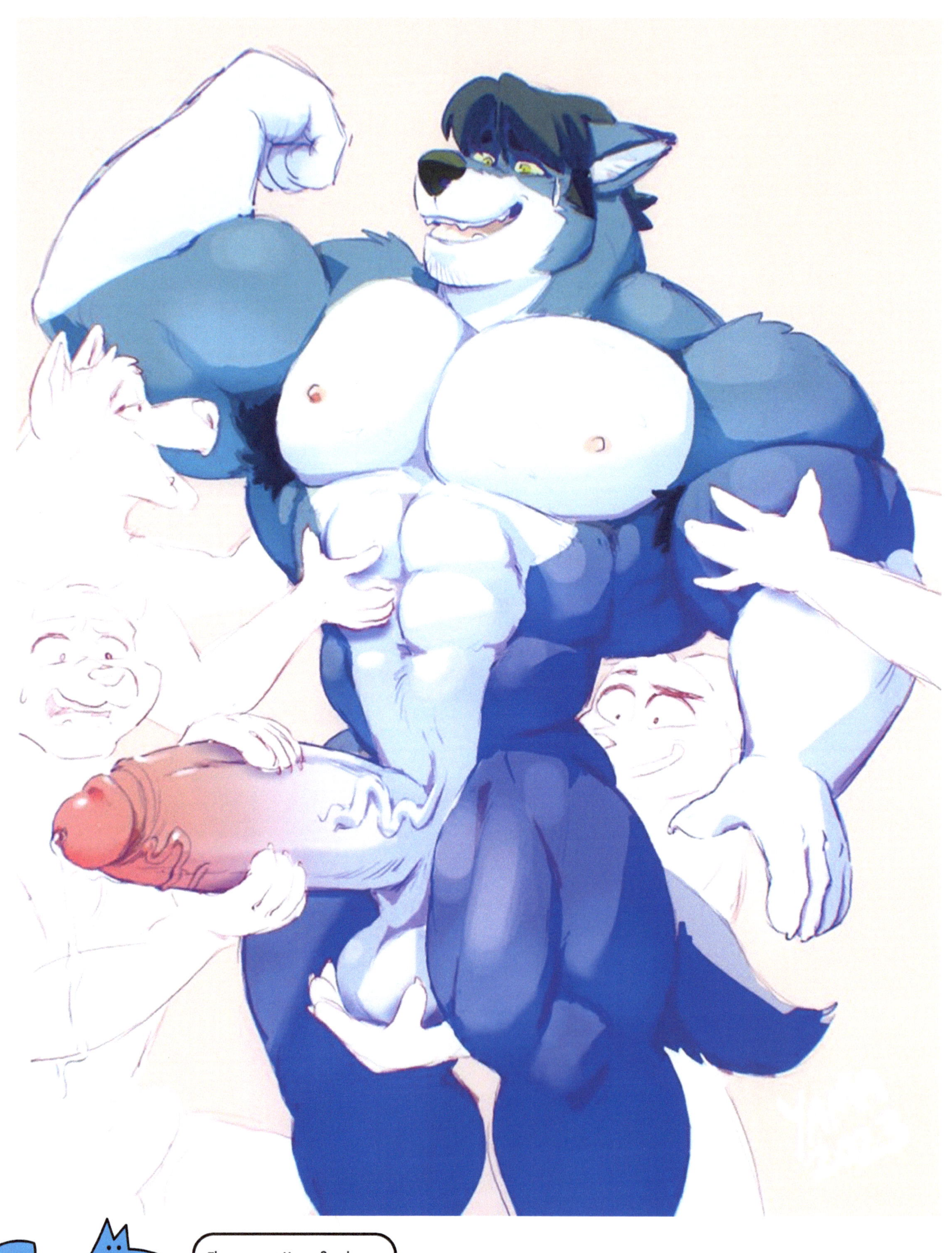
The moment Yama first learns
the joy of worship <:3

I wanna take you for a ride ~
funky jazz solo
I wanna take you for a ride ~

FUUUCK YEAaa, DUDE!
FEEL IT THROB IN YA?
OH FUCK
=PANT=
FEEL IT STRETCH YA OPEN?
I AINT EVEN CLOSE TO DONE WITH YA YET...
YAMA 2023

SPLOOSH

OH SHIT! OH FUCK!
I'M SO SORRY!
SHIT!
I-IT JUST
I FORGOT TO WARN YOU...
ARE YOU OK?
FUCK IT WONT STOP!!
...CAN YOU JUST GET ME A TOWEL?
DID IT- DID IT GET IN YOUR EYE?!
I'M SORRY!!
ZZZ
It really stings to get YOGURT in your eyes.
13

FUCK YEA!
WANT A HUG?
YAMA 2023
YAMA 2022
He really wants a hug but there's something in the way...
14

OH, THE WAIVER?
YEA.
THAT'S JUST THERE TO REMOVE ME FROM LIABILIT IN CASE YOU SUFF ANY INTERNAL INJ AS A RESULT OF AN AND ALL ACTIONS FRO NOW AND UNTIL THE 24 HOURS. NOT EXCLUDIN ANY LASTING EFFECTS FRO
...JUST TRUST ME. YER GUNNA HAVE FUN.
Don't just click thru the terms and conditions!! Really read them!!!

Look, I know I'm kinda shaggy rn... u still wanna hit it?
YAMA 2024
Unkempt, ungroomed, unemployeed, but definitely not unfuckable tbh.

Two bros chillin' in a hot tub
5 feet apart cuz they're not
gay~

THE FULK?!... AM I...? GROWING???

An American werewolf in... America? Eh, whatever.

UHHH...
NO. SORRY. I DON'T DANCE.
HEY! BACK OFF, BRO!
KLICK!
LOL WUT??
OF CURSE I DANCE!
YAMA 2023
Cats don't dance? Wait. Yes they do. Dancing with wolves?? What??

DUDE. WTF?
IK. COOL, RITE?

Yama does really well on Penis Inspecting Day. Almost too well actually.

WHY WON'T YOU GO DOWN?!
FUUUCKK!
jerks off god that was so hot *jerks off* fuck that was good too *jerks off*...
21

Y'ALL -- *SNORT* Y- Y'ALL GOT ANY PBRs?
YAMA
Hide yo cheap beers, hide yo beer pong, cuz were-bro Yama is crashing every party!

HURRRR...
WOBBLE
WHEN CAN I
GO HOME TO MY
FAMILY...?
YAMA
2024
A good quality footstool is so
hard to find these days...

A wild ELIAS appeared!
24

WATCH IT, BRO!!
THEY'RE SENSITIVE...
Not Fragile. 
Handle with un-care.

YIFFY

An AU where Yama grows out his hair. That's it. That's the AU.

YOU

THIS SHIT IS GETTING OUT OF CONTROL...
AWOOO!
SKRTCH!

Wow that was a fun idea.
Time to completely abandon it :)

I wish I could make this image scratch and sniff

KLAAANG

GRRRR!! ....

HELL YEA!

Anyway, Here's Wonderwall.

BRO, THIS AIN'T CUTE!
Put me down already...
D'AWWW... BUT YER SO ADORABLE ♥
YAMA 2023
Is it really possible for a Nirvana Wolf and a Slipknot Jock to be in a Bromance?

KLAAAAAAANG!!

FUCK YEA BRO!

LET'S FUCKIN GO!!

Get ready.
Yama's gonna
PUMP. YOU. UP.

I've watched years of anime
and the only thing I got were
these crummy speedlines

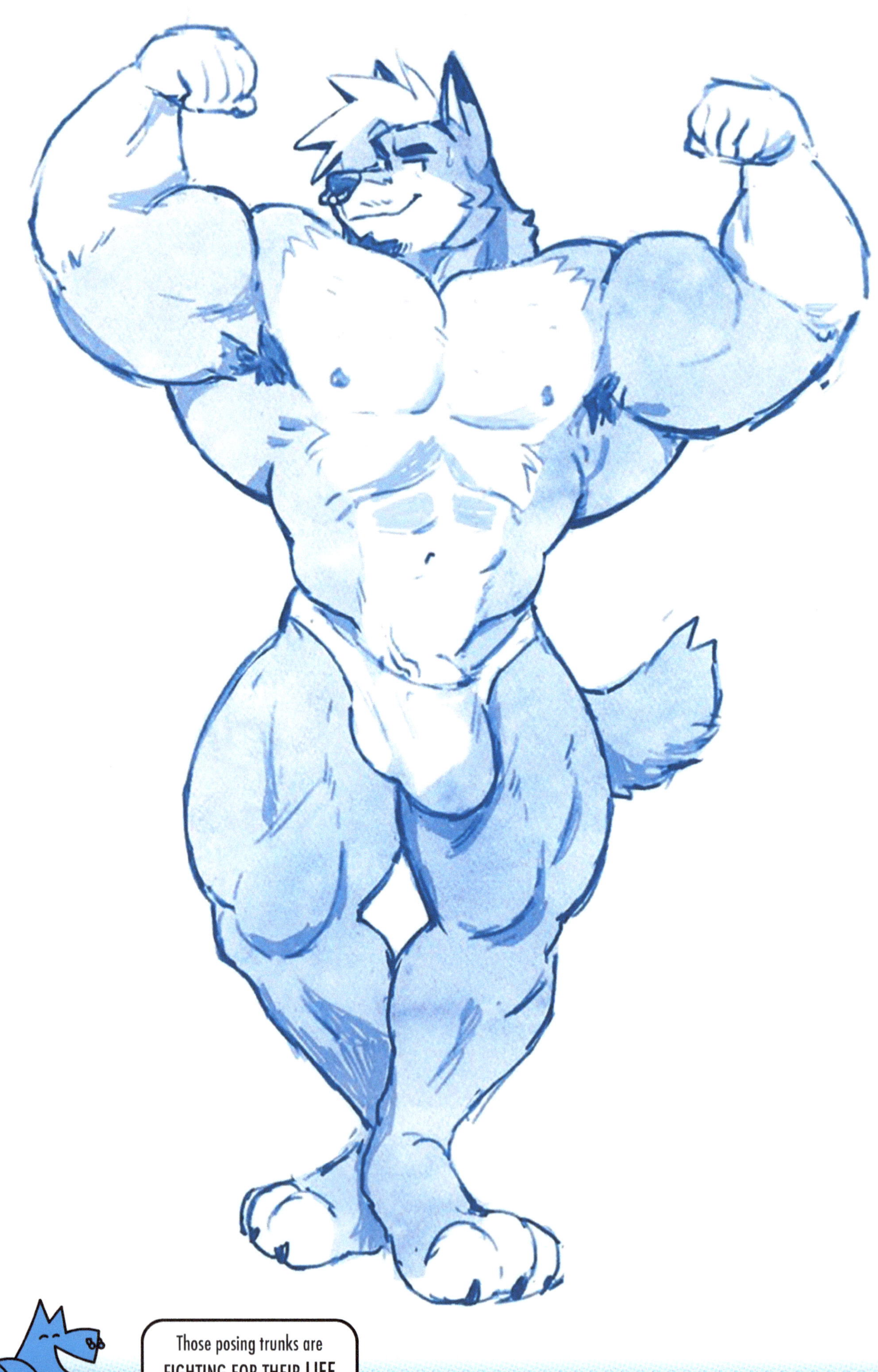

Those posing trunks are FIGHTING FOR THEIR LIFE

FUCK YEA...
420
420

Lore unlocked: After his career in bodybuilding, Yama takes up coaching.

OOPS! FORGOT TO GRAB SOMETHING FROM MY LOCKER
...FOR REAL?
YAMA 2024
Y-YER GOOD, BRO! TAKE YER TIME...

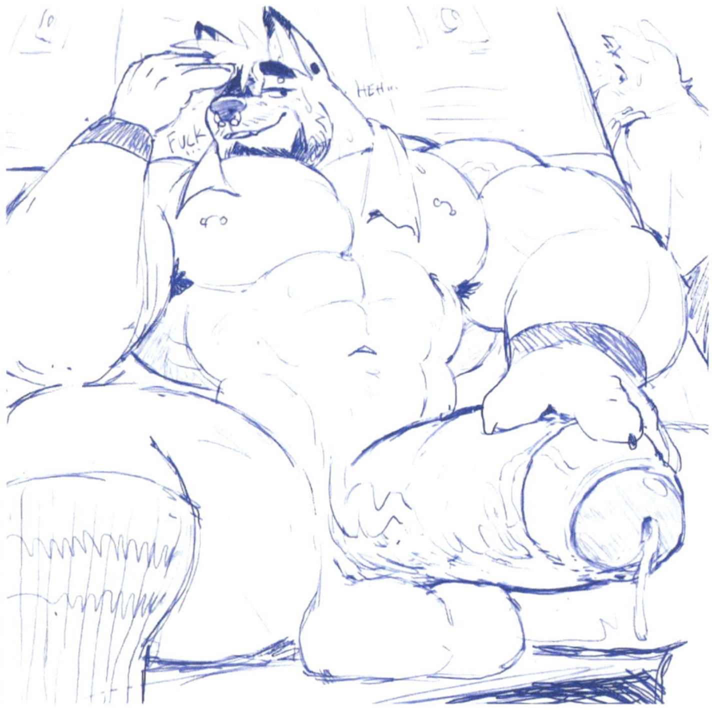

HEH...
FULK

HOLY SHIT DUDE...

BRO, YESSS!!

Just a lil lockerroom fun,
No Homo
Unless... ;)

BIGGER STRONGER HEAVIER
MASSIVE HUGE GROWING
HUNGRY CONSUME MEAT
TOWERING HULKING BEAS
MORE BEAS
MORE
BIG
YAMA
2024
Don't get too obsessed. Take
a break, take care of your-
self, drink lots of water.

HNNNNM
!!!
GAY
KLANK
KLANK

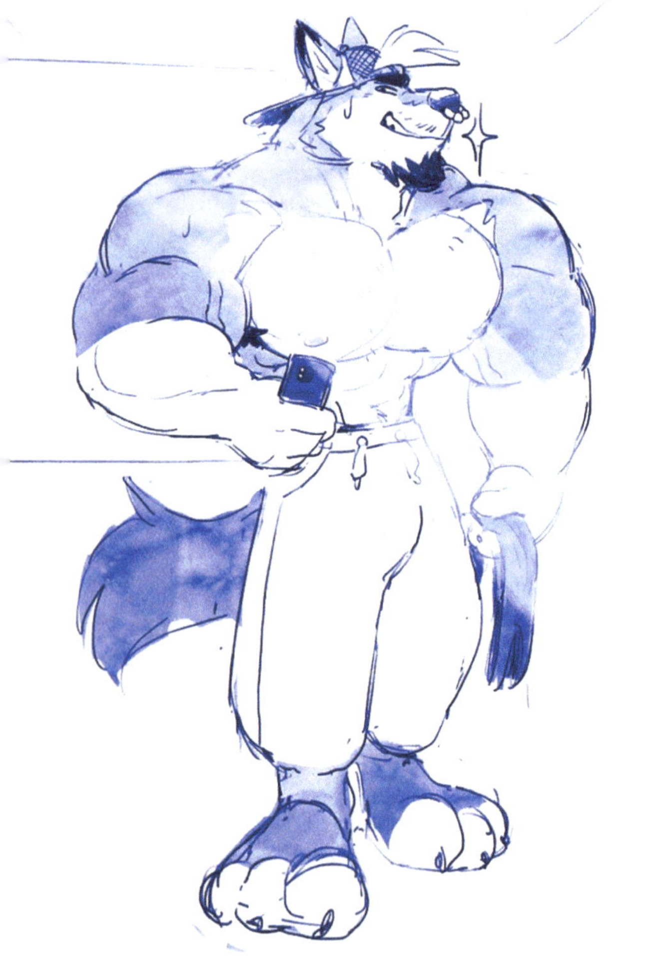

MAYBE...
...MAYBE HE
WON'T NOTICE
GOOD
LORD...

Great work out there, time for
a cool down! In the Sauna!
Cool off in the Heat!

DOOONT WORRY 'BOUT SPILLIN', DUDE. JUST CONCENTRATE ON GUZZLING DOWN AS MUCH AS YOU CAN
I GOT 5 OR 6 MORE LOADS JUST LIKE THIS.
PLAP!
PLOP!
Let's hit those showers! With high pressure fluids!

OH~ I AM GOD'S MOST PERFECT LI'L ANGEL
I STUDY THE HARDEST
ANGEL TRAINEE DWUDS
AND PRAY THE MOST
PLEASE GOD IT WOULD BE SO FUCKIN' FUNNY
AND HAVE COMMITTED MYSELF
TO SPREADING GOD'S INFINITE LOVE
Fig leaf doing a lot of work here.
40

AND TODAY..
I'M ON A MISSION STRAIGHT FROM GOD HIMSELF!
TO DELIVER THIS PARCEL TO THE KING OF THE UNDERWORLD
PAFF!
DEMON KING YAMA
I love his gay little purse so much. So much that I forgot to draw it in the last panel.

WHAT DOES GOD WANT NOW?!
GRRR..
GLANCE

HMM...

HA!

GYR HA HA!
DEMON KING YAMA, PLEASE ACCEPT MY GIFT OF MY MOST USELESS, MOST PATHETIC ANGEL. HE IS FAR TOO HORNY TO KEEP IN HEAVEN
DA G MAN

You don't have to laugh THAT hard. Ok, but it IS a little funny, huh?

HEH, THANKS FOR DA NEW TOY, GOD.
THANK YOU, GOD. THIS IS THE BEST GIFT YOU HAVE EVER BLESSED THIS LITTLE BEAR WITH ♥
PLAP PLAP PLAP!
OHHH...
DEMON KING'S TOY
YAMA 2023
Mission Accomplished.

Slaps Dwuds's butt
This bad boy can fit so much yogurt in him.

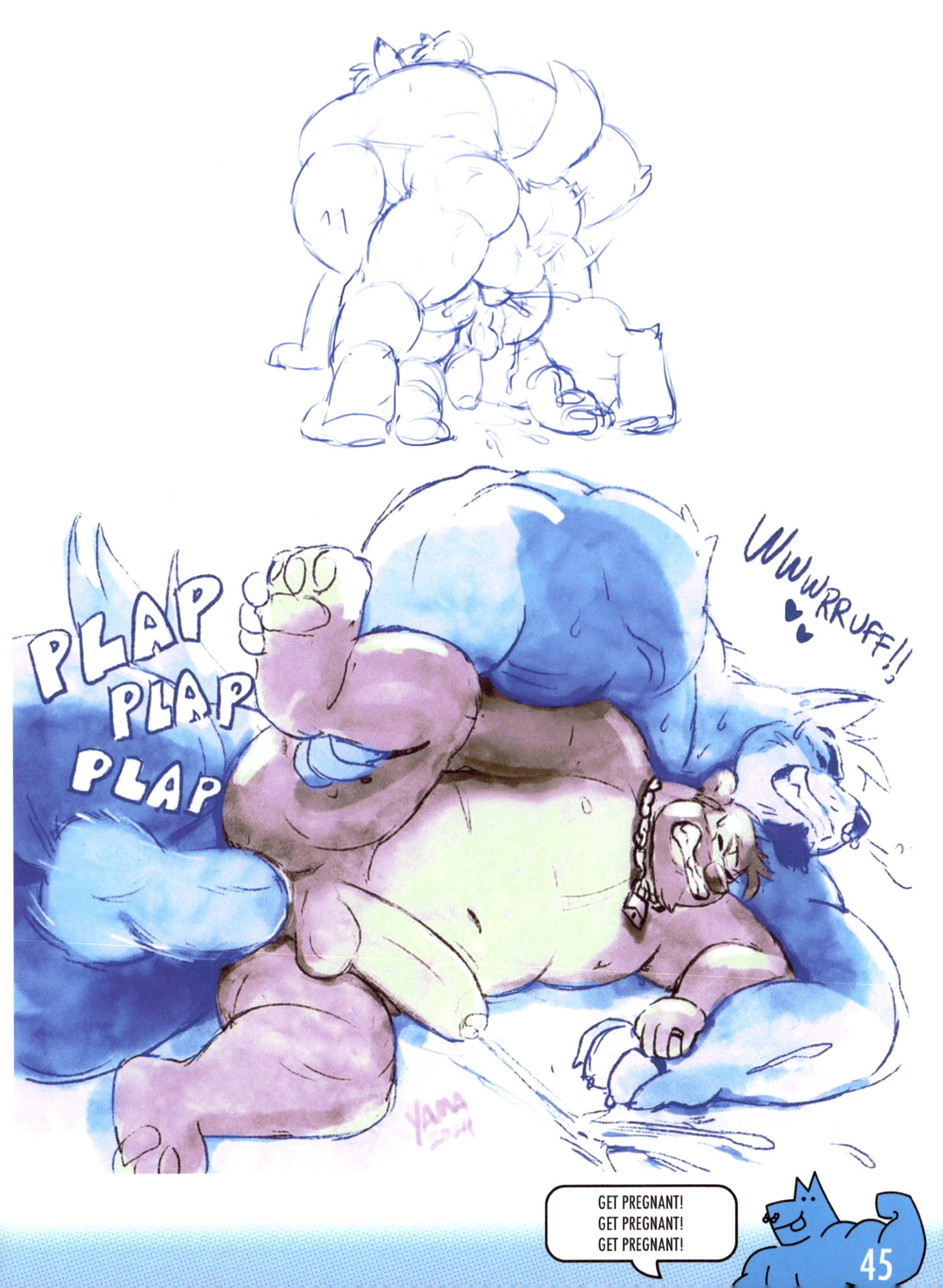

PLAP
PLAP
PLAP
WWWRRUFF!!
GET PREGNANT!
GET PREGNANT!
GET PREGNANT!

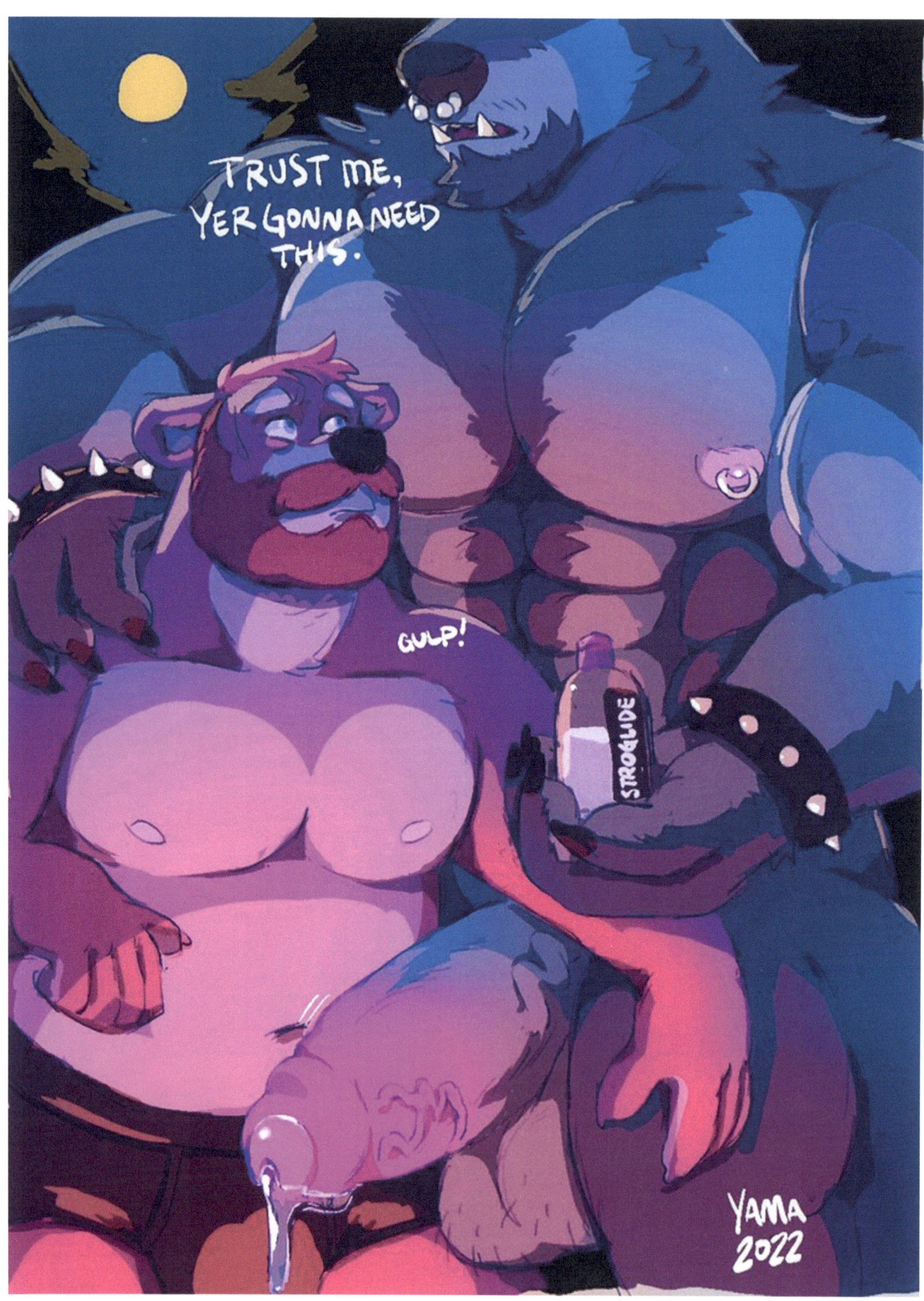

TRUST ME, YER GONNA NEED THIS.
GULP!
STROGLIDE
YAMA 2022
Oh how convenient! He carries around his own lube!
46

FUCK YEAAAA...
Q: What's Yama's favorite 
PS2 Classic?
A: Gape Escape 3
47

I'M GONNA GIT HARD
IF YA KEEP SNIFFIN ON MY
JUNK LIKE THAT

Love is stored in the balls
<3

AM I...
AM I DOING
IT RIGHT?
NO,
BUT I
THINK YOU
WON'T FIT
IN FRAME
ANYWAYS...
Love that guy.

OK, ENOUGH OF THAT GAY
LOVEY DOVEY SHIT. BACK TO
HARDCORE BUTTSEX!!

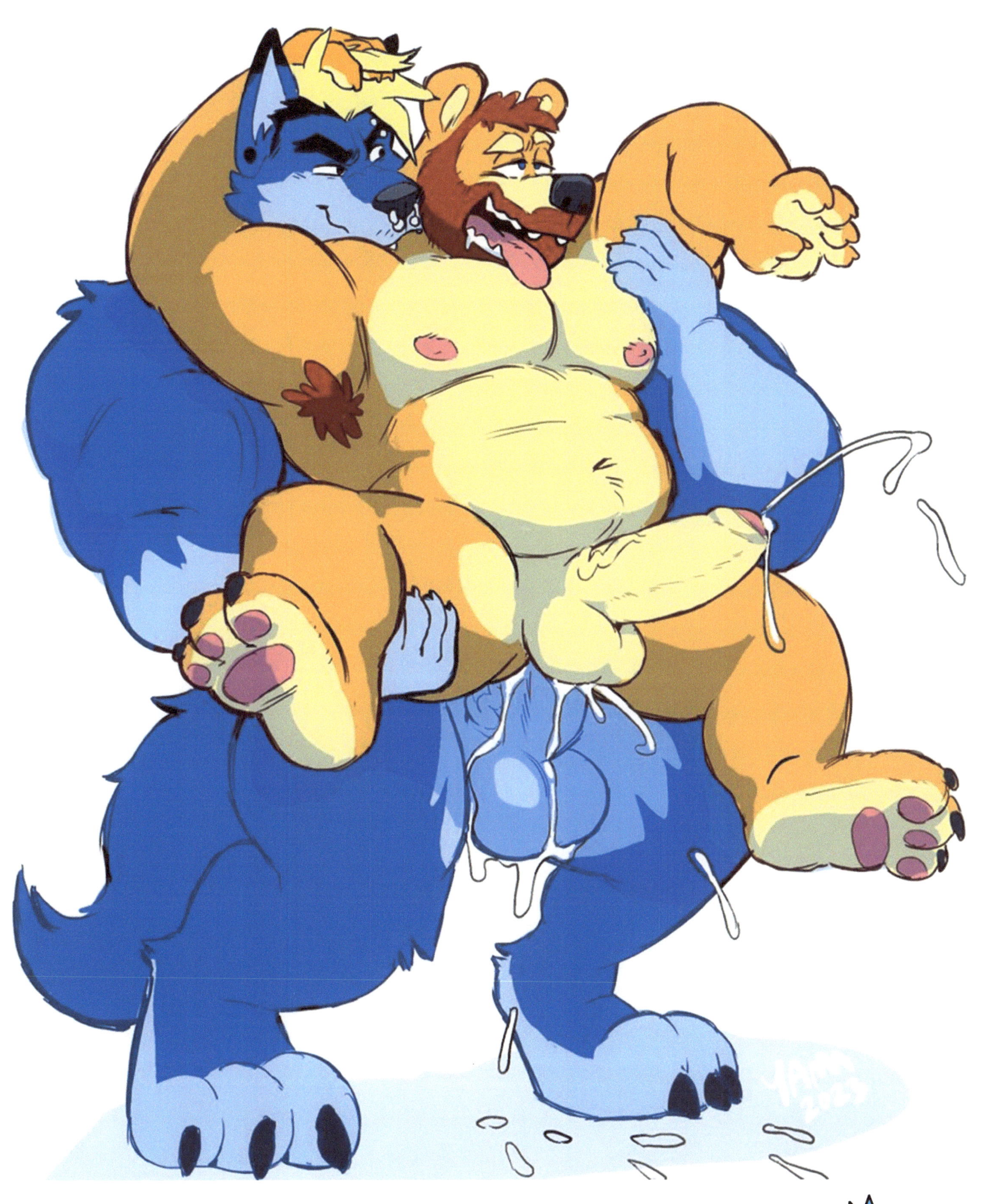
CHOMP!

One
Two
Three <3

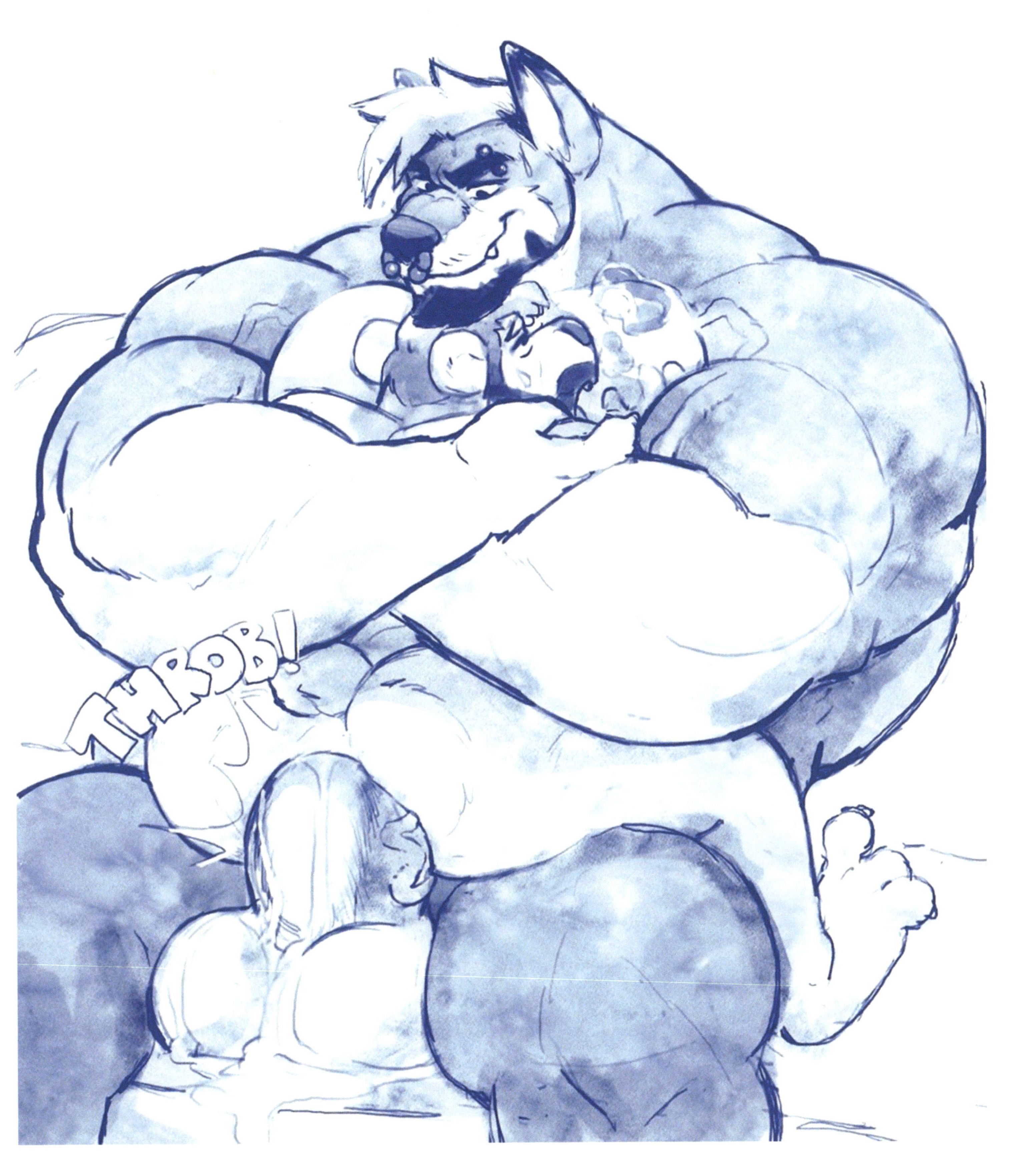

A tight hug, inside and out.

I... DIDNT EVEN GET IT IN ALL THE WAY

Don't worry, Yama. He can keep going.

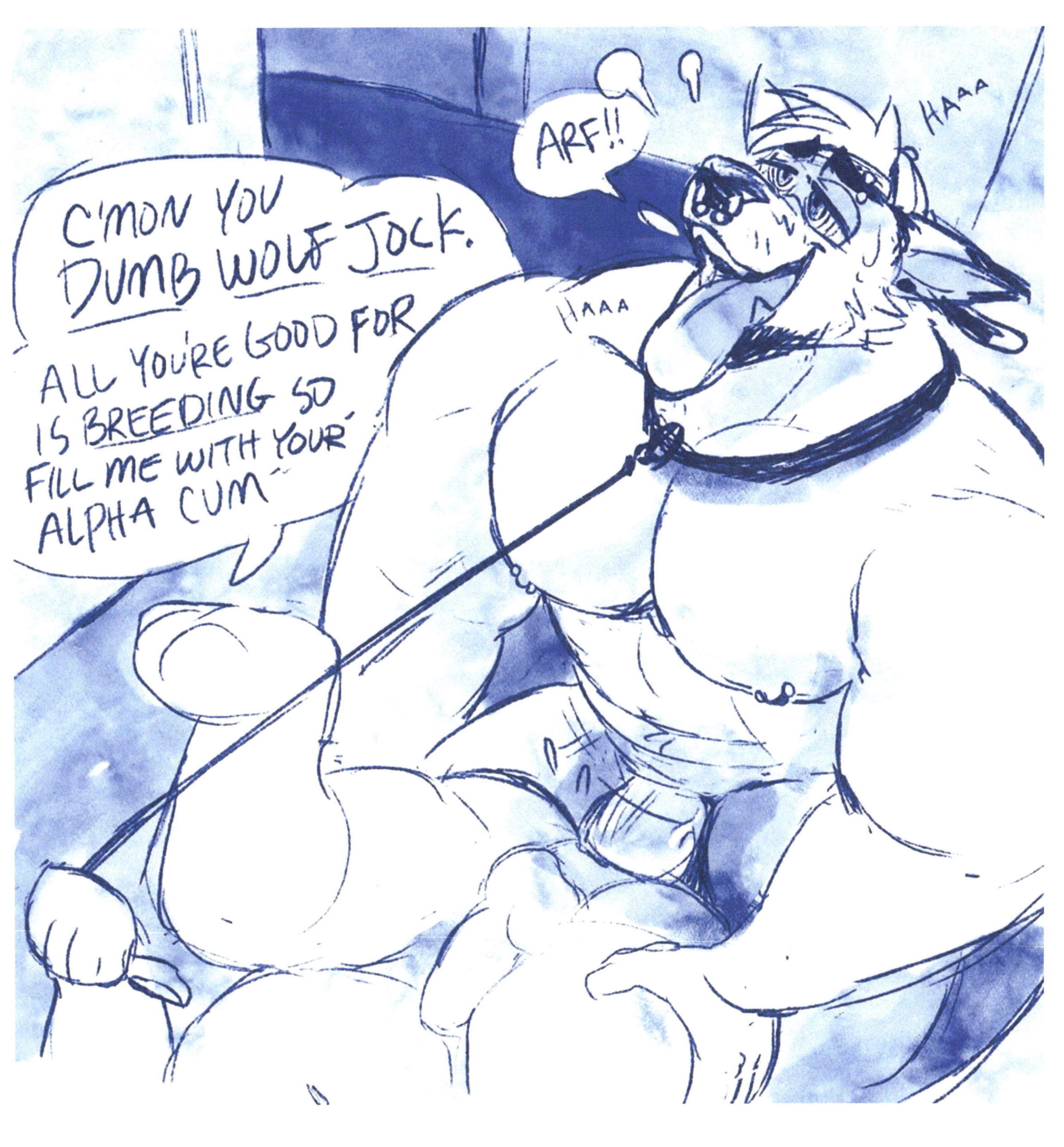
C'MON YOU DUMB WOLF JOCK.
ALL YOU'RE GOOD FOR IS BREEDING SO FILL ME WITH YOUR ALPHA CUM~
ARF!!
HAAA
HAAA
Arf?! <:3

I JUST THOUGHT OF SOMETHING
YEA?
WE'RE STREAMING MUSIC FROM YOUR PHONE, BUT...
BACK IN THE "Y2K" YOU'D PROBABLY BOOT UP YOUR RUROUNI KENSHIN SKINNED WINAMP PLAYER...
AAA...
AND PLAY MUSIC THRU YOUR PC'S SPEAKERS
HAHA, YEA
IMAGINE ONE OF YOUR BUDDIES STARTS IMing ABOUT THE LATEST CHAPTER OF NARUTO OR WHATEVER WHILE YOU WERE TRYIN' TO FUCK. LIKE,
BOO BEE BEEP!
OR EVEN JUST THE DOOR SOUNDS TBH
HAHA YEA, BUT... IMAGINE NUTTING TO THE
YOU'VE GOT MAIL!
VOICE.
OMFG.
YAMA 2021

Can't wait to get the seniors discount at movie theaters. It's expensive nowadays!

RRRGH!~
AAAAAAHH!!
PANT
FWUMP!
OH FUCK
PANT
WHAT?
PANT
PANT
PANT
OH! THAT'S JUST THE GALAXY STAR PROJECTOR I SET UP. YOU KNOW THE THING THEY ADVERTISE UNDER VIRAL TWEETS?
HIGH AS BALLS
OOOOOHH...
I CAME SO HARD, I'M SEEIN' STARS.
...

Yeah I enjoy a
Weed and Breed.

THERE'S A SHADOW IN THE GALAXY PROJECTOR

OH. THE SNAKE PLANT IS IN THE WAY...
OHHHH.. YEA.

ARE THEYYY... YOU KNOW...
PFFT!

GRRRR...
'DIS PANSY-ASS SNAKE PLANT IS BLOLKIN' MY VIEW!
DON'T BE HOMOPHOBIC TO OUR PLANTS...

Are they... Y'know?
derogatory hand gesture

FUUUCK
YOU CUMMIN' AGAIN???
Y-YEA.
SPLOORT

YOU CAME 4 TIMES HANDSFREE...
THEN ANOTHER 3 ON TOP OF THAT...
IS THAT A NEW RECORD ???
YEA

HA HA I SHOULD GET THE HIGHSCORE TATTOO'D, LIKE A TRAMP STAMP.
LMAO

I MEAN...
1ST SCORE NAME X8 YAM
THEN I'LL HAVE TO KEEP BREAKING THE RECORD

PET ME!
PET ME!
SAD AWOOS
PET MEEEE!!
I CAN PET YOU LATER! I'VE GOT AN IMPORTANT MEETING!
I REALLY WANT TO PET YOU!!
CONFLICTED BEAR NOISES
RRFF!!
AWFF!!
WIGGLE
HAVE YOU BEEN A GOOD BOY?
BIG PUPPY...
The price of having a wolf husband who is actually just a puppy husband.

Smooch
GRWD =ξ
Smooch
Love you to the moon and back, bear.

Coney meets Yama

A good D&D buddy is worth their weight in gp.

OW, YAMA! GENTLE!
HOLY SHIT HOLY SHIT HOLY SHIT SHIT HOLY
GNAW
GNAW

He had dumps like a truck, truck, truck. Thighs like what, what, what~

Oh...
He's down BAD.

SORRY TO DRAG YOU OUTTA THE PARTY BUT...
BRO...
I THINK I'M FALLING FOR YOU...

Hat's off.
That means it's serious time.

B-BRO...?!
YAMA
2024

Oh fuck oh fuck oh fuck oh
fuck oh fuck oh fuck oh fuck
oh fuck oh fuck oh fuck!!!

VMMM...
I GOT U
CHOCOLATE
+
FLOWERS,
BRO.
WHEY
DOUBLE
CHOCOLATE
HEY ARE
THOSE MY
NEIGHBOR'S
ROSE--
HEY WHAT
HAPPENED
MY ROSE BUSH
YAMA
2024

Bro doesn't know how to do
Valentine's Day.

Two himbos figure it out somehow.

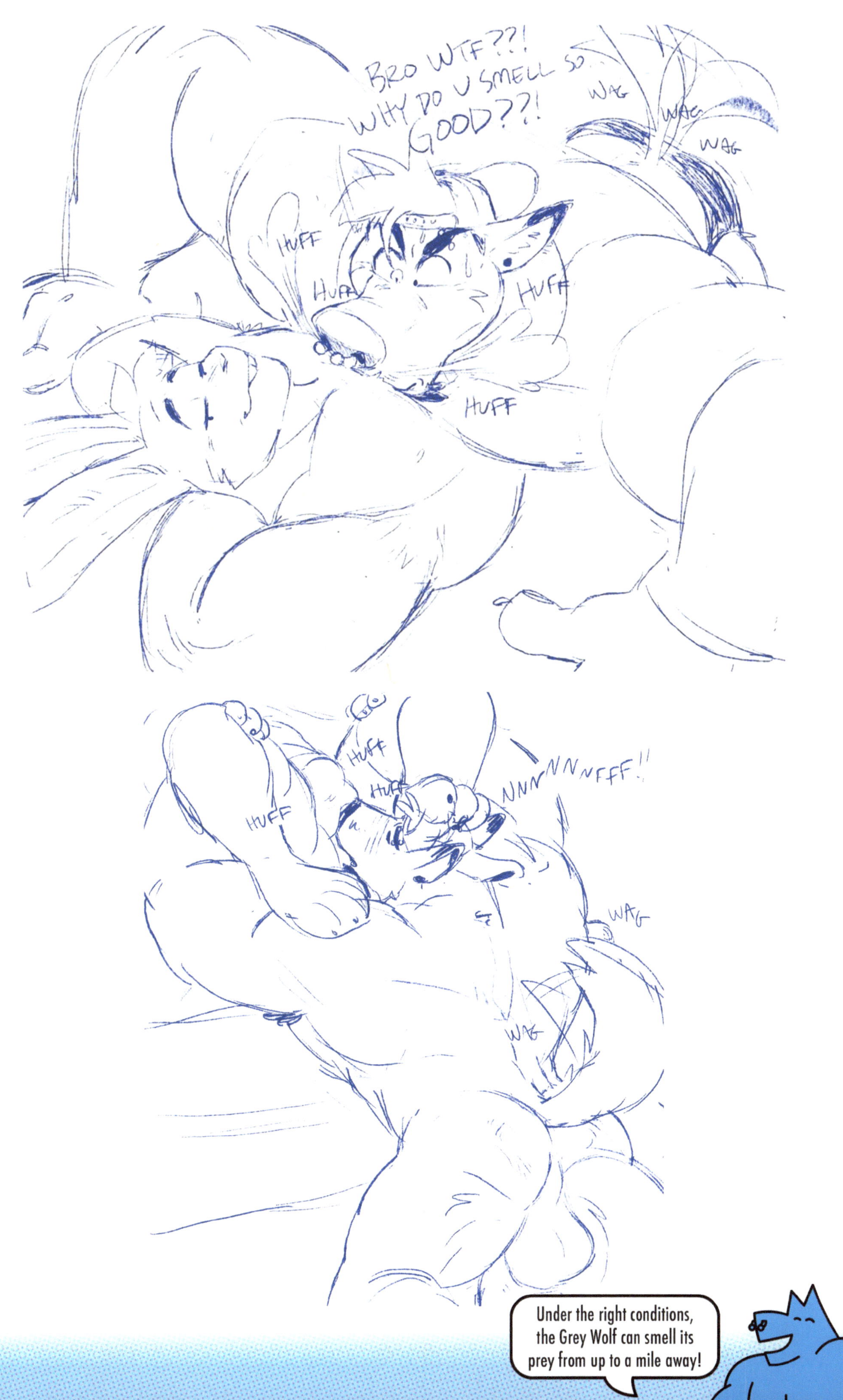

BRO WTF??! WHY DO U SMELL SO GOOD??!
WAG
WAG
WAG
HUFF
HUFF
HUFF
HUFF
HUFF
HUFF
HUFF
HUFF
NNNNNNNFFF!!
WAG
WAG
Under the right conditions, the Grey Wolf can smell its prey from up to a mile away!

HUFF
HUFF
HUFF
HUFF
HUFF
HUFF

Sniffty nining.

ARRGLRRR...
RIIIIP
FUCK!
SORRY, IT'LL BE OVER
IN A MINUTE...
ARF...
GULP
GLK...
YAMA
2024

Sorry if I wreck your couch,
bro.

HREH HEH HEH... BNNUY...
HUFF
OH FUCK
HUFF HUFF
YAMA 2024
Let your instincts take over.

Hop on it, bunny bro!

IT'S... WAY TOO BIG ON ME.
YA BRO... YOU CAN TRY ON ALL MY GEAR BUT...
YAMA'S HARNESS
FWUMF!
...I'M JUST BIGGER THAN YOU...???
AHEM YOU WERE SAYING?
UHHHH... NEVERMIND, BRO.
YOU CAN, UH, YOU CAN KEEP THAT BTW...
YAMA 2024

Oh, he actually fills in Yama's gear pretty well actually!

G'night, bro <3

NYEH HEH HEH
YOU FORGOT YOUR ARMOR, DOOFUS!
READY FOR AN ADVENTURE LIL BUDDY?
I JUST WANT HIM TO RAIL ME
Oh dude 4 strength 4 stam leather belt AUUGGHHH!! Level 18? AAGGHH OOOGHH!!

How do these horny were-
wolves keep getting
captured???

Y-YA MIGHT WANNA BE CAREFUL W'THAT
BY THE GODS!
IT'S SIMPLY TITANIC!
THROB!
WOAH!!
GRKK!
H-HOLD ON LIL BUDDY!
BUMP
OHHHH
EEP!
Barbarian Yama has a very unnecessarily high CHA stat.
78

LIL BUDDYYYY!!

GRAAH!!!

SNARL

'TIS NOT WHAT IT APPEARS!

Poor fox-bard lol.
He'll write heroic songs about
this encounter.

AAAH...
GRAHHH!!
I HATE FIGHTER'S FUCKIN' GUTS, BUT HIS DICK... ♡
CUMMING SO SOON?? I ONLY JUST STARTED!!
Giving new meaning to the phrase "Party Bottom"

All Hail Demon Lord Yama!
All Hail Demon Lord Yama!
All Hail Demon Lord Yama!

HEH...
WHAT NOW?

Uhh yeah I took 3 level of rogue to
get Fast Hands and 5 in fighter for
Action Surge and Extra Attack so
with an offhand attack I can...

The alchemist knows the best way to procure his secret ingredient is with a lot of praise

Oh! Um... Looks like you're busy. I'll just... I'll just come back another time.

CHECK IT.
COOL, RITE?

SERVICE
TOP

=CLICK=

HUH?
UP-SIDE
DOWN?

SERVICE
TOP

OOOHH
RIGHT!!

HERE YA
GO! PERFECT!

Great. Now just step in front
of a mirror. You Clown. You
absolute Buffoon.

BRO.
bruh.
KOFF KOFF!
YOU OK DUDE?
DUDE WHAT
I'm ok bro.
AAWRROOOOOO~!

Hmmm ~ Where to stick this thing next?

They're taking my mayo over my dead body.

FUCK YEA DUDE
I AM YOUR ALPHA
WORSHIP MY COCK
YEEAAAAH GET MY PIT STINK ALL OVER YOUR HANDSOME FACE
I'LL MAKE YOU FEEL SO GOOD
CUM FOR ME
FUCKING CUM!
HEHEH... ARF! ♡
WAG WAG WAG
AWRARWAR ♡
RRFF! (PET ME)
WHIIIINE (I'M GONNA CUM!)
GENTLEMEN...
MEN WHO WHIMPER
Sometimes I'm daddy. Sometimes I'm puppy.

DUDE! YOU MAKE PIZZA BAGELS? BE A BRO + TOSS ONE IN HERE

WE'VE BEEN FUCKING FOR HOURS, I NEED A REFUEL.

AH~

When pizza's on a bagel you can have buttsex with the door open ANYTIME

Ask and ye shall receive.

ME? WEAR A COLLAR!? A PROUD, NOBLE WOLF?!
DAMN, IT DO LOOK GOOD THO...
YAMA

WHINE
WHIMPER
FLOP!

How quickly the mighty have regressed into puppy head-space.

ARF!
(TL's note: arf means plan)
Just according to arf.

Gimme PETS...
GOOD BOY!
AWWW~ YER JUST A...
VERY LARGE PUPPY,
HUH?
mm-Hm!
NO!
GOOD BOY!
Pet pet pet your pet gently on the chin. Merrily merrily merrily merrily. Life is but a dream.

HMM...
PUP-GRO
GUARAVITE GROWTH!
NOT FOR ADULT CANINES
MEH!
SHRUG
DOESN'T KNOW HOW TO READ
!!
RIP!
SPLOOSH

If OOPS ALL YAMAS was a real cereal, I think it should do this.

Oh hey, we're near the end of the book! Thanks so much for reading up until now.

YO... RELAX, BRO.
...YA STILL WANT THIS?
Y-YES!!
SO-SORRY, I JUST--!!
GOOD.
--MMPH!
YO, YOU GOOD?
...YES~

I'm so grateful for all my fans and supporters who have encouraged me to keep drawing

YOU DO NOT NEED TO BE A CERTAIN SHAPE!
EXERCISE? YES! EAT HEALTHY? YES!
PRESSURE YOURSELF TO FIT INTO WACK BEAUTY STANDARDS? NO!!

I KNOW IT SEEMS LIKE EVERYWHERE YOU LOOK IN CERTAIN GAY SPACES, ONLY A FEW BODY TYPES GET ADMIRATION...
BUFF DOG FACTORY
OH MURR
OH MURR
OH MURR
PSSSH!
OH FUCK!
... BUT MUCH OF THAT IS A REFLECTION OF WHAT IS POPULAR FOR PORN. DON'T LET THAT WARP THE WAY YOU SEE YOURSELF & OTHERS. IT IS FAKE.

WHAT IS REAL THEN? YOUR RELATIONSHIP WITH YOURSELF IS WAY MORE IMPORTANT THAN ANY PHYSICAL TRAIT
BEING SECURE IN WHO YOU ARE IS NOT A SEXY MARKETABLE IDEA THAT GETS A TON OF VIEWS/LIKES.
BUT REAL PEOPLE NOTICE.
(DESPITE MY MUSCLE FETISH I LIKE ALL KINDS OF BODIES IRL.)
YAMA 2023

And I hope that in some small way, my art makes a difference to you all.

BODY IMAGE

I THINK IT'S GREAT AND PLAIN FUN TO BE A PART OF A SEXUALLY OPEN AND EXPRESSIVE COMMUNITY BUT...

... A LOT OF ATTENTION GOES TOWARDS THOSE WHO ARE VERY MUSCULAR AND MASCULINE PRESENTING...

... AND LEADS MANY INTO THINKING THAT THEY ALSO NEED TO FIT THAT MOLD AT ALL COSTS

ALL I CAN SAY IS, I KNOW DEEP IN MY SOUL THAT THE STUFF I REGRET ON MY DEATHBED WILL NOT BE ANYTHING TO DO WITH MY APPEARANCE

I WILL BE THINKING ABOUT SPENDING MORE TIME WITH LOVED ONES.

ACCOMPLISHING THE WORKS I WANT TO MAKE

EXPERIENCING MORE OF WHAT THE WORLD HAS TO OFFER.

YAMA + DWUDS
in "ONE WEIRD TRICK"

And this is the end! I hope you enjoyed and treasure this book. Keep me safe!

SPECIAL THANKS

Although I've been creating art in the fandom for a while, I have (for the most part) done so as just a hobby. A very important and meaning-ful hobby to me, yet it was always seperate from my professional life. At the start of 2024 I got news that I was going to be laid off and immediately felt like it was a sign to try and make a way for myself out-side of the office environment that I felt was so stifling for so long.

A big thank you to my husband who has supported me through so much this year, as well as my close friends who keep me company on discord calls while I work at my desk. And thank YOU for helping to support me as I take this new step as an artist.

CREDITS

A big thanks to my friends who let me draw their characters

page 8 Blake – x.com/blueishhyena

page 30 ACIDWUFF – x.com/ACIDWUFF

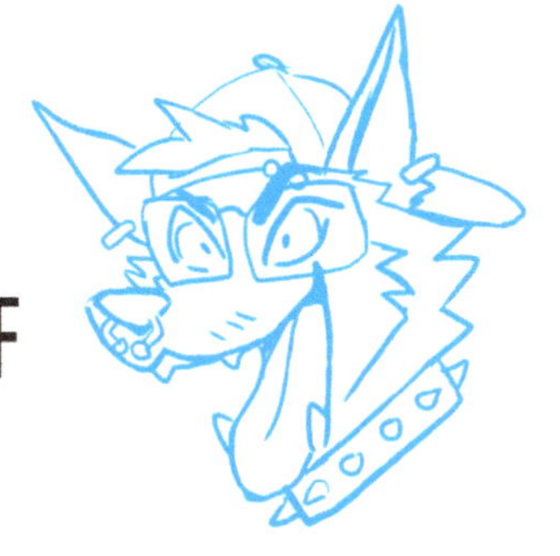

page 36 SizableDanger – x.com/SizableDanger

pages 40-61, 100 Dwudles – x.com/dwudad69

pages 62-75 Conejito – bsky.app/profile/conejito.bsky.social

page 100 Monty - x.com/xgay_ratx